# ONE DROWSY DRAGON

# BY ETHAN LONG

SCHOLASTIC

CLANG! CLANG! CLANG!

**ONE** marching dragon clanging on a cup.

One drowsy dragon mumbles,
"Don't wake me up!"

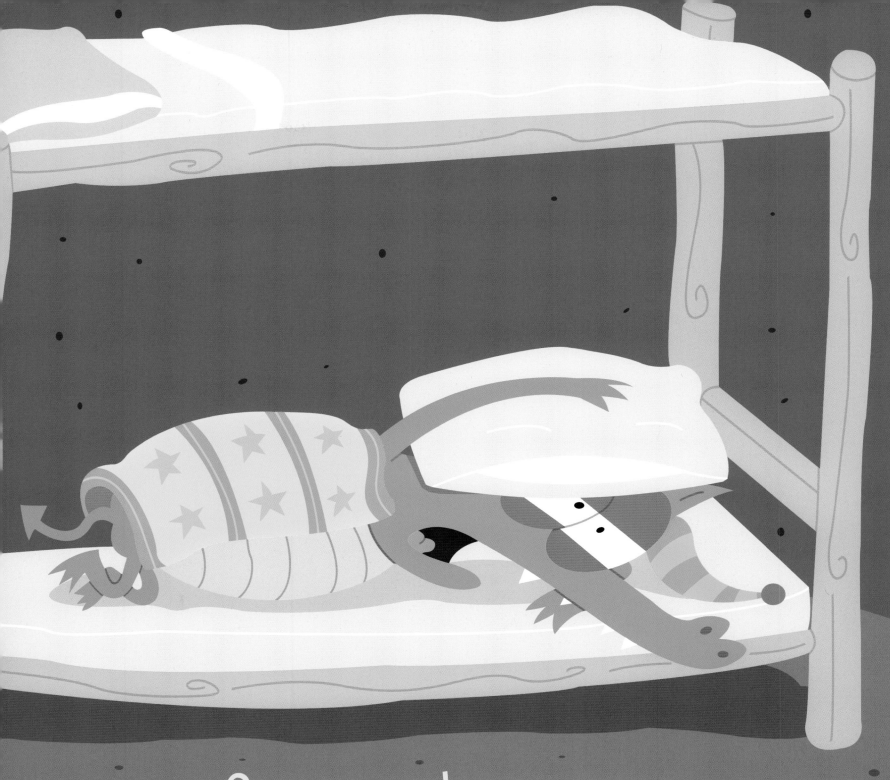

One weary dragon moans,
"Please let me sleep!"

# THREE dancing dragons
## learn to tap, tap, tap.

One groggy dragon groans,
"I want to nap!"

One tired dragon asks,
"Please keep it down?"

# FIVE laughing dragons
## dump their games and toys.

One grumpy dragon growls,
"Too much noise!"

One cross dragon yells,
"I am still awake!"

SEVEN screaming dragons
watch a scary show.

One loud dragon shouts,
"I'm tired! Don't you know?"

# EIGHT rambunctious dragons all play croquet.

One fed-up dragon shrieks,
"This I cannot stand!"

One weary dragon
rests his sleepy head.

One drowsy dragon finally snores deep.

Ten drowsy dragons say....

For Cooper, my idea guy.
Love, Dad ~ EL

First published in 2010 by Scholastic Inc
This edition first published in 2010 by Scholastic Children's Books
Euston House, 24 Eversholt Street
London NW1 1DB
a division of Scholastic Ltd
www.scholastic.co.uk

London ~ New York ~ Toronto ~ Sydney ~ Auckland
Mexico City ~ New Delhi ~ Hong Kong

Text copyright © 2010 Ethan Long
Illustrations copyright © 2010 Ethan Long

ISBN 978 1407 12080 5